Arthur and the 1,001 Dads

A Marc Brown ARTHUR Chapter Book

Arthur and the 1,001 Dads

Text by Stephen Krensky
Based on a teleplay by Peter K. Hirsch

LITTLE, BROWN AND COMPANY

New York ✦ An AOL Time Warner Company

First Edition

The characters and events portrayed in this book are fictitious. Any
similarity to real persons, living or dead, is coincidental and not intended
by the author.

Arthur® is a registered trademark of Marc Brown.

Text has been reviewed and assigned a reading level by Laurel S. Ernst,
M.A., Teachers College, Columbia University, New York, New York;
reading specialist, Chappaqua, New York.

Library of Congress Cataloging-in-Publication Data

Brown, Marc Tolon.
   Arthur and the 1,001 dads / Marc Brown.
      p. cm. — (Marc Brown Arthur chapter book ; 28)
   Summary: Arthur and his friends try to find a substitute to attend the
Father's Day picnic with Buster, whose father is not around much since
his parents' divorce.
   ISBN 0-316-12516-4 / ISBN 0-316-12280-7 (pb)
   [1. Aardvark—Fiction. 2. Animals—Fiction. 3. Fathers—Fiction.
4. Divorce—Fiction.] I. Title: Arthur and the one thousand-one dads.
II. Title: Arthur and the one thousand-and-one dads. III. Title.

PZ7.B81618 Af 2003
[Fic]—dc21   2002069354

10   9   8   7   6   5   4   3   2   1

WOR (hc)
COM-MO (pb)

Printed in the United States of America

For my sister, Kim,
a.k.a. D.W.

Chapter 1

● ● ● ● ● ● ● ● ● ● ●

Arthur, Francine, and D.W. were looking at a poster for the Father's Day picnic on the park bulletin board.

"It's on Sunday," said Francine.

"Just a few days away," said Arthur. "I've been dreading it all week."

Francine frowned. "But I thought you loved that picnic."

"I do," Arthur insisted. "I love the pie-eating contest and the sack race and especially the egg toss."

"He never wins any of them," said D.W. "That's how you can tell he really loves it."

"I might win this year," said Arthur.

D.W. just laughed.

"I've been practicing," Arthur told her.

"Okay," said Francine, "then why are you dreading the picnic?"

Arthur sighed. "Because of Buster. The picnic is a hard time for him. I mean, it's the *Father's Day* picnic. And Buster's father isn't around like everyone else's. Remember last year? Buster didn't even show up."

"Oh, yeah," said Francine. "He told us he had a cold or something."

Arthur nodded. "That's what he said, but he didn't look sick. And he didn't sound sick either. I'll bet he was just embarrassed that his dad was away, and if he went, he wouldn't have a partner for the games. Imagine in the egg toss if he had to throw and catch the eggs by himself." Arthur shuddered at the thought.

"Or maybe," said Francine, "he was afraid someone would find out that his parents are divorced."

"Big surprise," said D.W. "Who doesn't know that?"

"Lots of people," said Arthur. "It's not like Buster ever advertised it."

"*Sssssh!*" said Francine. "Look who's coming."

It was Buster. He waved and walked over to join them.

"Hi, guys," he said. "You all look so serious."

"Actually," said Arthur, "D.W. was just telling us a joke."

"I was?" said D.W. "I don't remember that."

Arthur poked her. "That's because it wasn't a very good joke."

"I see you're looking at the picnic poster," said Buster.

"Poster?" said Arthur. "We hadn't noticed."

"Really?" Buster looked surprised. "It's right behind you. Anyway, I know how

much you look forward to the picnic, Arthur."

"Even though he never wins anything," said D.W.

"All right, all right," said Arthur. "That's not important. What *is* important is that everyone comes and has a good time."

"Absolutely," said Buster.

"You agree?" asked Arthur.

Buster nodded. "Couldn't agree more."

"Great! Then you'll be coming this year?"

Buster hesitated. "Well, no, I can't, actually. I've, um, got other plans."

"Other plans?" said Arthur.

"You know, Buster," said Francine, "I just remembered. . . . My sister can't come this year, so we'll be one kid short in my family. Why don't you come with us?"

"Thanks, Francine. I appreciate it. But like I said, I'm busy."

"Busy?" said Arthur. "With your *other plans?*"

"Yup. Well, I have to go. See you guys around."

He walked off.

Arthur and Francine shared a look and shook their heads. Buster's situation was just as bad as they thought.

Chapter 2

• • • • • • • • • • • •

That night at dinner, Arthur didn't do much eating. While everyone else was cutting and chewing and swallowing, he just kept stabbing at his mashed potatoes.

"You know, Arthur," said his father, "I think you're worrying too much."

"Huh?" Arthur looked confused.

"About your mashed potatoes, I mean," his father explained.

Arthur still looked confused. "I'm not worried about my mashed potatoes," he said.

"Really? The way you're poking at

them, I thought you were afraid they might clump up on you."

"Oh." Arthur put down his fork. "Sorry."

Mr. Read smiled. "You don't have to apologize to me. I'm not the one being poked."

For just a moment, Arthur looked like he might apologize to his potatoes. Then the moment passed.

"Is everything okay, dear?" asked his mother. "Any problems at school?"

"Nope. School's fine."

"So nothing's bothering you?"

Arthur could feel his face reddening.

"Tell them," said D.W.

"Be quiet!" said Arthur.

D.W. looked at her parents. "Then I'll tell them. Arthur's upset about Buster and the Father's Day picnic."

Arthur poked his potatoes again.

"The Father's Day picnic . . . ," Mrs. Read repeated.

"Ahhhhh," said Mr. Read. "I think I understand. Is it possible that Buster's father will not be around on Sunday?"

Arthur nodded.

"I see," said Mr. Read.

"It's not fair," said Arthur.

"You're a good friend," said his mother, "to care about Buster's feelings like that. Is he doing all right? What does he say about it?"

"He just pretends it doesn't matter," said Arthur. "He's making excuses to cover up. But I can tell what he's really thinking."

"Being in a divorced family isn't easy," said his father. "There are new feelings and situations to juggle. And not only are there challenges inside the family, but things come up — like the picnic — that relate to most other kids."

"Divorce seems like a lot of trouble," said D.W.

"Well, it is," said her mother. "But some-

times, when a mother and a father don't get along anymore, it's the best thing to do. Not a happy thing, you understand, just the best thing."

"If you ask me," said D.W., "what Buster needs is another father, someone who could be around more."

"That's silly," said Arthur. "Dads aren't like babysitters. You can't just get a new one when your regular one is busy."

"*Hmph!*" said D.W. "You're just mad because you didn't think of it first."

"I think you're forgetting something, D.W.," said Mr. Read. "Buster still has a father. And they still love each other. But since Buster's father is a pilot, he travels a lot and can't always be around."

"So those of us who are around," said Mrs. Read, "can sometimes help fill in the gaps."

"But what can I do?" asked Arthur.

"Two things," said his mother. "First, start eating those mashed potatoes. And second, just be there when Buster needs you. That's one of the best things a friend can do."

Chapter 3

. . . .

The next day, at the Sugar Bowl, Arthur and Francine were still thinking about Buster.

Arthur sighed. *"Be there when he needs you,* my mother said."

Francine took a sip from her milkshake. "That's good advice, I guess. But kind of boring."

"I know. I keep remembering how Buster looked when he walked away. It was so sad. I wish we could do something for him."

"Didn't you say D.W. had an idea?" asked Francine.

Arthur frowned. "Which one? D.W. has so many, I try to block them out."

"The one about getting Buster a new dad?"

"No, no, that would never work. As I told D.W., you can't just hire someone to be a new dad."

"Wait a minute, Arthur," said Francine. "I mean, we're not talking about getting a new dad to last forever. What if we got someone to be Buster's dad for a day? You know, just to fill in."

Arthur considered it. "That might work. But who would we get?"

"It can't be just anyone," said Francine. "We need somebody guaranteed to be a lot of fun at the picnic."

Arthur nodded. "Somebody who knows lots of jokes . . ."

"Somebody who can impress the kids," Francine added.

They were silent for a moment.

"Are you thinking what I'm thinking?" asked Arthur.

"I don't know," said Francine, "but I'm certainly thinking what I'm thinking."

"A clown!" they said together.

"Clowns are funny," said Francine. "Buster would like that."

"And a clown would laugh at his jokes, no matter how bad they were."

At that moment, the door opened and the Brain came in.

"Hi, guys," he said. Then he gave them a long look. "You know, even from here I can see your wheels spinning. What's up?"

They told him about Buster's problem. Then they explained their idea.

"So you think a clown is the answer?" said the Brain.

"A really good clown," Arthur pointed out.

The Brain shook his head. "Your aim is

admirable," he said, "but you haven't fully considered the psychology of the matter. Why do you think Buster wouldn't go to the picnic by himself?"

"Because he'd stick out," said Francine.

"Exactly," said the Brain. "You think he's worried about sticking out because he'll be there without his dad. But if he's there with a clown, he'll stick out, too. In fact, it will be worse. A clown will stick out like a sore thumb. Nobody else's dad looks like a clown. So not only will his dad not be there, he'll also be the only kid walking around with a clown."

"Well, it *seemed* like a good idea," said Arthur.

"And you're on the right track," said the Brain, "but what you need is someone who would fit in. Someone who would look like a real dad."

"But where will that someone come

from?" asked Francine. "We don't have much time."

"Leave it to me," said the Brain. "I have an idea."

Chapter 4

• • • • • • • • • • •

"I don't know why the Brain couldn't just tell us his idea," said Francine.

"Maybe he wants to surprise us," Arthur said.

They were standing in the park. The Brain had said he would meet them there, but had to go home and get a few things first.

Francine looked at her watch. "Well, I was ready to be surprised twenty minutes ago. Now I'm just ready to go home."

"Give him a little longer," said Arthur. "He had that look in his eye. Whatever he's planning will be worth the wait. Look, here he comes now."

The Brain was approaching slowly, pulling a wagon behind him. Something was in the wagon, something heavy by the way the Brain was pulling on the handle. But they couldn't see what it was because a sheet was covering it up.

"Sorry I'm late," said the Brain, "but I had to adapt this from a project I was already working on. It took a little longer than I estimated."

"So, what is it?" said Francine.

With a flourish, the Brain pulled off the sheet.

"Wow!" said Arthur.

There, curled up in the wagon, was a life-size, fully dressed robotic man holding a folded newspaper.

"Lady and gentleman, say hello to RALF, the world's first *Remote Automated Lifelike Father*."

"Does *he* or *it* work?" asked Francine.

"Watch." The Brain took a remote control from his pocket and pressed a button. The robot immediately unfolded itself from the wagon and walked over to a bench. There, it sat down, crossed its legs, and opened the newspaper.

"Amazing!" said Arthur.

"RALF will make a perfect companion for Buster at the picnic," said the Brain.

"They have to meet first," said Francine. "How do you plan to arrange that?"

"All taken care of," said the Brain, tapping the side of his head. "I asked Buster to meet us here."

"Oh, look!" said Francine. "He's coming."

Buster was approaching in the distance. Arthur, Francine, and the Brain hid behind a tree to wait.

As Buster passed by the bench, the Brain pushed a button, and RALF stood up. The Brain pushed another button.

"*Meow, meow,*" said RALF.

"Oh, no!" the Brain whispered. "I was in such a hurry I forgot to replace the recorded cat voice."

Buster looked at RALF with concern.

"Are you okay, sir?"

"*Meow . . . meow . . .*"

"Uh-oh." Buster frowned. "That sounds serious. I hope you haven't swallowed a cat."

Buster went behind RALF and thumped him on the back. A button popped off RALF's cardigan sweater, revealing a spring.

Buster looked at RALF suspiciously. "Wait a minute . . ."

At that moment, the Brain, Arthur, and Francine rushed out from behind the tree.

"Hey, Buster!" said the Brain. "Just trying out my, um, new toy. Oops! I guess this is broken."

"But . . . ," Buster began.

"Sorry, Buster. Science waits for no man. Come on, Arthur, Francine. Help me get him, er, *it* back in the wagon."

"Yeah," said Arthur. "We'd better go fix it."

As they shuffled off, Buster stared after them, shaking his head. "Sometimes," he said to himself, "science can be very strange."

Chapter 5

• • • • • • • • • • • •

The following day in class, Arthur and Francine tried to figure out their next step.

"So robots are out," said Arthur.

"Definitely," Francine agreed. "Too unreliable."

Arthur nodded. "We need someone we can depend on, someone rock solid, an anchor in the —"

"I get it, I get it," said Francine. Suddenly, her eyes focused on the front of the room. "What about . . ."

"Who?" said Arthur.

Francine kept staring. "Wouldn't he be perfect?"

Arthur followed her gaze. "You're not serious?"

"Time's running out, Arthur, and we don't exactly have applicants lining up around the block."

"Well, he *is* used to being around kids," Arthur admitted.

"Exactly!" Francine smiled. "Come hand in your homework — and follow my lead."

They walked up to Mr. Ratburn's desk and put their homework down on the pile he was grading.

"It's too bad Buster has no one to go to the picnic with," said Francine.

"How true," Arthur added. "If only some nice grown-up with no kids of his own would take him."

Francine smiled. "Yes, that would be a perfect solution. How clever of you to think of it."

As they returned to their seats, Mr. Ratburn arched an eyebrow. He had always had such a good time at the picnic years before with his own father.

Old Father Ratburn sat on a blanket, stroking his beard as he illustrated a math problem to his five-year-old son. All around them, kids were playing with hula hoops or doing tricks with their yo-yos, but the little boy's attention was fixed on his father.

"Listen carefully," said Old Father Ratburn. "If Obadiah had four persimmons and Esther took two for herself and two for Ezekiel, how many would Obadiah have left?"

"None," said the five-year-old Ratburn.

"That is correct."

"May we do another, Father? One math problem is never enough. Please? Please?"

"Are you okay, Mr. Ratburn?" asked Buster, who was handing in his own paper.

"Hmmm? Yes, yes. Tell me, Buster, are you aware that the Father's Day picnic is fast approaching?"

"Um, yes."

Mr. Ratburn cleared his throat. "As it happens, I don't have anyone to go with. Would you care to join me?"

Buster blinked a few times.

Mr. Ratburn was sitting with Buster near a campfire. The other kids were off playing games, but Buster was just sitting.

"Mr. Baxter, your attention, please," said Mr. Ratburn. He showed Buster a marshmallow on a stick.

"You see," he explained, "the skin of the marshmallow turns brown through the process of carbonization."

Buster looked longingly after the other kids. He wondered if he could join them for just a few minutes.

"You should be taking notes on this, Mr. Baxter. There will be a test tomorrow."

"Buster?"

Buster looked back at Mr. Ratburn. "Oh. Well, thanks for asking, but luckily — I mean, I just happen to have other plans."

As Buster turned around, he noticed Arthur and Francine watching him. Then they hurriedly turned away.

"Hmmm," said Buster. Even if he hadn't been one of the world's greatest detectives, he would have known something was up.

Chapter 6

· · · · · · · · · · ·

Buster stood on Arthur's doorstep and rang the bell. He thought he heard noises inside, but he couldn't be sure.

The door opened a little, and Arthur poked his head out. "Yes?"

"I'm glad you're home, Arthur," said Buster. "Everyone is acting really weird around me, and —"

"Sorry, Buster. I can't talk now."

"You can't? Why not?"

Arthur hesitated. "Well, I'm really busy."

"Oh. Is there any way I can —"

"No, no," said Arthur. "Thanks, but

there are some things you can't help with. You understand, don't you? Good. Bye."

He closed the door.

Buster frowned. It seemed like Arthur was acting a little strange. *Very* strange, actually. He rang the doorbell again.

Arthur's head poked out again. "Yes? Oh, it's still you, Buster."

"Yes," said Buster, "it's still me. Are you all right?"

"Of course I'm all right," said Arthur. "Why do you ask?"

"I don't know. You seem a bit jumpy."

"Well, of course. After all, I have to keep getting up to answer the door."

"Ah," Buster said, nodding. "Okay. I just wanted to say that if you think I'm upset about Father's Day, you don't have to be —"

"Don't you worry," Arthur interrupted. "Father's Day is going to be great.

Spectacular. Stupendous. I promise. Can't talk more now, though. Bye."

He closed the door again.

Buster sighed and started back toward home. Arthur was certainly free to work on a project without his help. Buster just wished he could be more sure that Arthur had heard a word he said.

Inside Arthur's living room, there was a moment of silence.

"Is he gone?"

"That was close."

"Too close."

"*Sssssh*," said Arthur. "Buster has good ears."

He was speaking to Francine, Muffy, Binky, and the Brain. They had gathered to come up with a solution to Buster's problem. But they hadn't gotten very far.

"Buster looked really sad," Arthur went

on. "The picnic is the day after tomorrow. What's left? We've tried a robot. And we're are all out of grown-ups."

"What about a kid?" asked Binky.

"What do you mean?" Arthur asked.

"You said you can't think of any more grown-ups to substitute for Buster's dad. But a kid could still do it."

"Who?" asked Muffy.

"Me," said Binky.

"You?" said Francine.

"Well, I'm older," Binky explained.

"Only by one year," said Arthur.

"That may be true," Binky admitted, "but I'm also bigger."

"I'm not sure that's enough," said Francine.

"It might work," said Muffy. "Binky doesn't have to do this on his own. We could train him."

"But why would you volunteer, Binky?" asked Arthur.

Binky smiled. "Fathers get to boss their kids around, don't they?"

"I guess," said Arthur.

"That's good enough for me. Besides, I don't see a lot of other fathers lining up for the job."

Arthur looked at Francine. "What do you think?"

"I don't see a lot of other ideas lining up either," she said. "I guess it's worth a shot."

Chapter 7

At the library, Binky sat at a long table, reading. He looked up as the Brain and Arthur carried over a big stack of books.

"Whew!" said Arthur. "I had no idea being a parent was so complicated."

The Brain nodded. "The factors and variables are certainly numerous. In any case, these are all the library's books we could find on being a parent."

"Thanks, guys," said Binky. "And tie your shoelace, Arthur. You know, that can be dangerous. You could trip on it and fall. As for you, Brain, don't stand there with your mouth open like that. You'll catch flies."

"He seems to be getting the hang of it," the Brain noted.

That night, Binky went over to Muffy's to get his new wardrobe. Muffy had collected a tweed jacket, a button-down shirt, dress pants, argyle socks, and shiny leather shoes.

Binky eyed the clothes warily. "Some of this stuff looks itchy," he said.

"I suppose so," said Muffy, "but it will be a high-quality itch because this is a very high-quality wool."

Binky frowned. "They look uncomfortable, too."

"Don't sound so surprised," Muffy reminded him. "These are grown-up clothes, after all. They're supposed to be itchy and uncomfortable. Anyway, you need to get dressed." She looked at her watch. "The test begins in a few minutes."

"Test?" Binky looked confused. "What test?"

"We're not letting you loose on Buster until we see what you've learned."

"Nobody said anything about a test," Binky grumbled.

"Hey, this was your idea, remember? Oh, there's the doorbell. That must be everyone else."

"Everyone else?"

"Of course," said Muffy. "I'm not doing this alone. You try on the clothes, and then we'll get started."

"But . . . but . . ."

"Move it!" Muffy ordered.

A short time later, Binky sat in a wing chair in the living room. Facing him were Muffy, Arthur, Francine, and the Brain.

"Gee, Binky, you almost look distinguished," said Francine. "Who would have guessed?"

"Although," the Brain added, "the effect is diminished every time he scratches."

"I can't help it," Binky moaned.

"On with the questions," said Muffy. "All right, Binky, here we go. Number one. Your son wants to watch TV, but he still has homework to do. What do you say?"

Binky took a deep breath. "Watching TV is a privilege, not a right. Do your homework first."

"I'm next," said Francine. "You tell your child to take out the trash, but she keeps forgetting. What do you do?"

"Collect all the trash in the house and put it in her room. That way she'll remember for sure."

"How about this?" said Arthur. "You're

40

tucking in your son for bed, and he says there's a monster in the closet."

"I'd open the closet door and tell the monster that if he dares to come out, he'll have to answer to me. Then I'd growl at him."

"Last question," said the Brain. "Your daughter is working on some quadratic equations but is having trouble isolating the variables. What would you do?"

"I'd call you," said Binky, "and have Uncle Brain explain it to her."

"So, judges," said Muffy, "what do you think?"

"Impressive," said Arthur.

"Distinguished," said the Brain.

"He's so good it's scary," Francine put in.

"All right, then," said Muffy. "Binky, the job is yours."

Chapter 8

● ● ● ● ● ● ● ● ● ● ●

The next afternoon, Binky and Buster met at the creek.

"Well, I'm here," said Buster. "What's all the mystery?"

Binky smiled. "All in good time, Buster, my boy." He took a deep breath. "Ah . . . smell that? It's the fresh air. Fresh air is good for you, Buster. It will help you grow."

"Okay, I guess I've heard that." Buster frowned. "But why are you dressed that way? It makes you look old."

"Does it?" Binky beamed.

"Those clothes look itchy, too," Buster

went on. "I'm surprised they don't bother you."

"My, my," said Binky, "what an imagination you have."

"And what about those glasses? Since when do you wear glasses?"

"Careful, Buster. Too many questions will put a permanent frown in your forehead. We wouldn't want that, would we? Of course we wouldn't. Now, I've brought fishing poles for our excursion. I also have refreshments."

Binky opened a thermos and handed Buster a cup. "Hot chocolate, my boy?"

"You're sure you weren't hit on the head or something?" Buster asked.

"Nonsense. I just thought it would be nice to have some quality time together."

Binky started to pour, but he was not used to looking though the glasses and spilled some of the hot chocolate.

"Ow!" said Buster. "Watch it! Why don't you take off those silly glasses?"

"They're not silly. And quit moving the cup, dummy." He paused. "I mean, watch it, my boy, this is a hot beverage."

"Binky, why do you keep calling me your boy?"

"Because it's . . . well . . . hold that thought." A look of panic crossed Binky's face. He quickly turned his back and started rifling though a copy of *How to Be a Parent*, which he had in his pocket.

Buster crossed his arms. "This is some crazy plan Arthur cooked up, isn't it? He wants to keep me from feeling like I don't have a dad."

"Um, yes. Don't get upset," said Binky. "You'll spoil your appetite for dinner."

"Stop giving me fatherly advice," said Buster. "You're not fatherly, and it's crummy advice."

"Hey!" Binky looked mad now. "Just play along, doofus! It's for your own good."

"I don't need you to tell me what's good for me and what isn't," Buster said.

"Don't talk to me in that tone of voice, young man."

"LISTEN!" Buster shouted. "YOU CAN TELL ARTHUR I ALREADY HAVE A DAD. I DON'T NEED ANOTHER ONE. AND I'M NOT SAD EITHER!"

He marched away.

Binky shook his head. "Yes, you are. You're miserable. Parents have a way of knowing these things. We . . . can . . . tell."

Binky stopped talking when he realized Buster was too far away to hear. *"Hmph!"* he said, throwing off his jacket. "Some son. I'll bet he won't even get me a tie for Father's Day."

Chapter 9

• • • • • • • • • • •

At the Sugar Bowl, Buster sat sipping a milkshake and reading a Bionic Bunny comic book. The story was just reaching the exciting part, but even so, he found it hard to pay attention. He was still mad about Binky. The milkshake, though, was helping a little.

He looked up as the door opened. It was Arthur.

"Hello, Buster," Arthur said quietly.

"Well, well," said Buster, "if it isn't the Dad Delivery Service. I wonder who my father will be today. Will it be the cashier? Or maybe that friendly mailbox outside.

Stay tuned. We'll be back after this message."

Arthur shook his head. "Don't worry, Buster. I get it. I've stopped trying to find someone to go to the picnic with you."

"Finally. So now you believe I have something else to do, right?"

"No," said Arthur, "but I've decided not to go either. I won't have a good time without you there. I'm going to spend the day with you instead."

Buster gasped. "No, no, no, no, no!"

"What do you mean?"

"Arthur, you *have* to go!" Buster insisted.

"I don't, actually. I'm sure my father would understand. Maybe not right away, I admit, but someday . . ."

"Look, Arthur, I appreciate the support," Buster continued, "but you don't want me to feel guilty that you didn't go, on top of everything else, do you?"

Arthur paused. "No. That would be terrible."

"Exactly," said Buster. "You know, Arthur, you're a really good friend."

"Um, thanks," Arthur said.

"I just wish your hearing was a little better."

Arthur frowned. "What's wrong with my hearing?"

"YOU DON'T ALWAYS LISTEN. Yes, sometimes I get upset that my parents aren't together. And once in a while, I just really want to see my dad and I can't. I have to call him instead."

Arthur nodded. "That must be hard."

"It is," said Buster. "But I really enjoy the time I do get to spend with him. And even though my parents aren't together, we're still a family. It's just different from yours. So you can stop worrying about me."

Arthur nodded. "Okay, okay. I'm glad

we got things out in the open. Sometimes you just have to clear the air."

"Air clearing is good," agreed Buster. "So promise me you'll go to the picnic. It's what your family is supposed to be doing."

"I guess. Still, it's going to feel funny. Why don't you come with us?"

"NO! HOW MANY TIMES DO I HAVE TO TELL YOU? I HAVE PLANS."

Arthur rolled his eyes. "Come on, Buster. You want me to be honest. You need to be honest, too! You keep mentioning these *plans*, but you never say anything more about them. I'm your best friend. If you really had plans, you'd tell me what they were!"

Buster eyed him slyly. "That's true. But as far as my plans go, you'll find out soon enough."

Chapter 10

● ● ● ● ● ● ● ● ● ● ● ●

"Careful, Arthur," said Mr. Read.

He spoke cautiously because he was about to throw Arthur an egg.

The Father's Day picnic was going strong. The sack race and tug of war were already over, and the egg toss was in its third round.

Mom, Kate, and D.W. were all holding their breath.

"Okay, Arthur! Here it comes! Get ready!"

Mr. Read lobbed the egg.

"I've got it," said Arthur. "I've got —"

SPLAT!

"Oops," said Mr. Read.

On the other side of the field, Mr. Ratburn handed a pair of binoculars to Tommy Tibble.

"And up there, in that tree, you can see a bay-breasted warbler of the genus *Dendroica*."

"My turn, my turn!" said Tommy's brother, Timmy. He grabbed the binoculars for a look.

"It's a dragon!" he gasped.

Tommy snatched the binoculars back. "That's no dragon. It's a UFO."

Mr. Ratburn took back the binoculars to see for himself. "Actually, it's not a dragon or a UFO. It's something far more unexpected."

"What?" Tommy and Timmy said together.

"It's Buster Baxter."

By now everyone was looking up and pointing. It really was Buster, leaning out from a hot-air balloon that was drifting down over the field.

"HAPPY FATHER'S DAY!" Buster shouted. "HAPPY FATHER'S DAY!"

Everyone looked amazed, but nobody more than Arthur.

The balloon continued to descend, finally reaching the ground. When it was safely tethered, the basket door opened, and Buster and his mother stepped out.

Arthur, Francine, Muffy, Binky, and the Brain came running up to him.

"Buster, this is incredible!" said Francine.

"Yup. My dad rented this thing for the whole afternoon. So everyone can have a ride. See, Arthur? I told you I was busy. And I wanted it to be a surprise. Now, who wants a ride?

"Me!"

"Me, too!"

"I want a ride!"

Only Arthur turned away.

"Arthur, what's wrong?" asked Buster. "Aren't you coming?"

Arthur turned back. "Of course. I wouldn't miss it for anything. But I have to get cleaned up first. I have egg on my face."

Buster smiled. "So you do," he said.